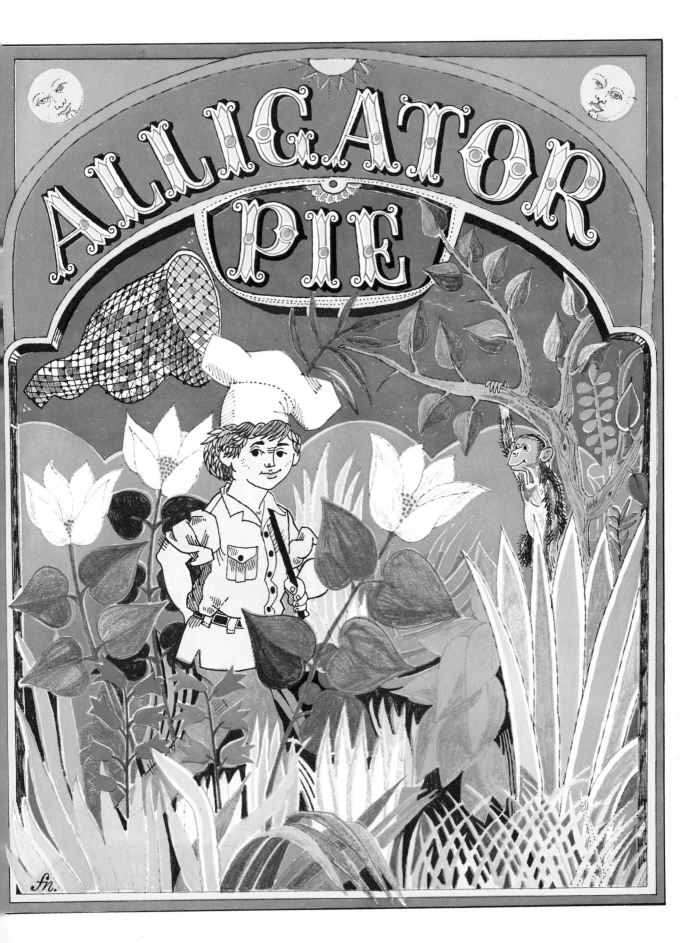

PIE the poems were written by DENNIS LEE

the pictures were drawn by FRANK NEWFELD

Macmillan of Canada
A Division of Canada Publishing Corporation
Toronto, Ontario, Canada

ALL RIGHTS RESERVED

Originally published in 1974 by The Macmillan
Company of Canada under ISBN 0-7705-1193-7

OOKPIK

1963 mark and copyright of Her Majesty
the Queen in Right of Canada, used herein
with the permission of the *Licensor* and in
association with Noel J. Walsh and Associates,
Exclusive Canadian Licensee for OOKPIK
publications.

The author is grateful to the Canada Council,
whose support helped him complete this book.
He is also grateful to the many people —
strangers and friends, young and old — who
contributed to the final form of the poems.

Canadian Cataloguing in Publication Data

Lee, Dennis, date.
  Alligator pie
Poems for children.
ISBN 0-7715-9591-3 bound   ISBN 0-7715-9566-2 pbk.
I. Newfeld, Frank, date.   II. Title.
PS8523.E3A84 1987   jC811′.54   C87-094188-7
PZ8.3.L43A1 1987

Eleven of the poems in this book, *Flying Out
of Holes, Ookpik, Willoughby Wallaby Woo, The
Fishes of Kempenfelt Bay, Skyscraper, Alligator
Pie, Kahshe or Chicoutimi, Street Song,
Holidays, Wiggle to the Laundromat,* and *In
Kamloops,* appeared in an earlier publication,
Wiggle to the Laundromat, published by
New Press. We are grateful for permission
to reproduce them here.

THIS BOOK WAS DESIGNED BY FRANK NEWFELD

· 13 14 15 16 17 18 AP 93 92 91 90 89 88 bound
  2 3 4 5 6 AP 92 91 90 89 88 87 pbk.

Macmillan of Canada
A Division of Canada Publishing Corporation
Toronto, Ontario, Canada.

Contents

for Kevin and Hilary

Alligator Pie

Alligator pie, alligator pie,
If I don't get some I think I'm gonna die.
Give away the green grass, give away the sky,
But don't give away my alligator pie.

Alligator stew, alligator stew,
If I don't get some I don't know what I'll do.
Give away my furry hat, give away my shoe,
But don't give away my alligator stew.

Alligator soup, alligator soup,
If I don't get some I think I'm gonna droop.
Give away my hockey-stick, give away my hoop,
But don't give away my alligator soup.

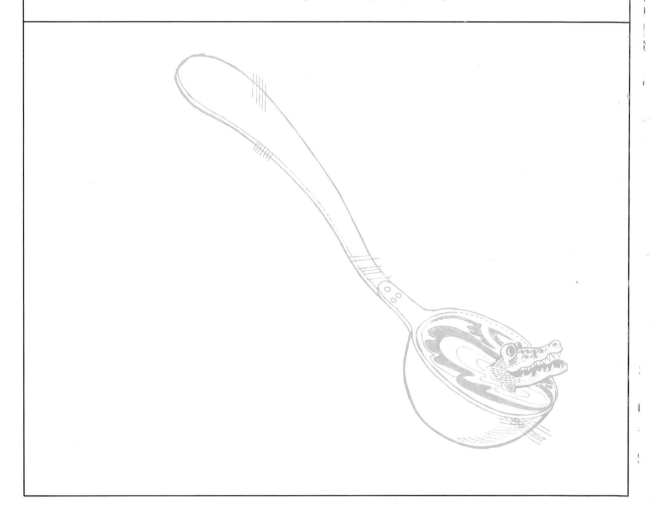

Wiggle to the Laundromat

Wiggle to the laundromat,
Waggle to the sea;
Skip to Casa Loma
And you can't catch me!

Singa Songa

Singa songa sea
I've got you by the knee.

Singa songa sand
I've got you by the hand.

Singa songa snail
I've got you by the tail.

Singa songa seat
And it's time to eat!

Bouncing Song

Hambone, jawbone, mulligatawney stew,

Pork chop, lamb chop, cold homebrew.

Licorice sticks and popsicles, ice cream pie:

Strawberry, chocolate, *vanilla!!!*

Street Song

Sidewalk,
Hippity hop,
Step on a crack
Or you can't come back.

Skippity one,
Skippity two,
Wait for the mailman
And kick off your shoe.

Mumbo, Jumbo

Mumbo   Jumbo
Christopher Colombo
I'm sitting on the sidewalk
Chewing bubble gumbo.

I think I'll catch a WHALE…
I think I'll catch a *snail*…
I think I'll sit around awhile
Twiddling my thumbo.

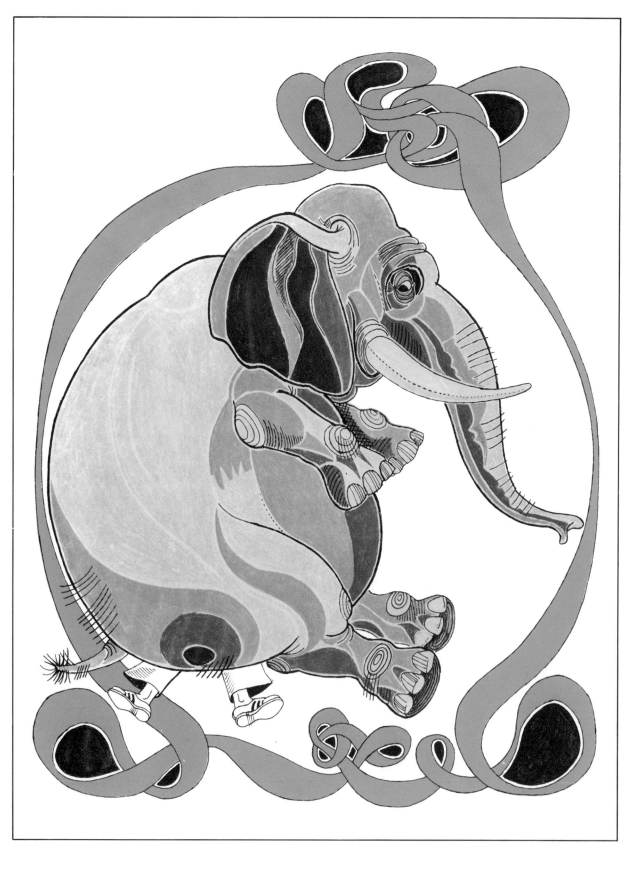

Willoughby Wallaby Woo

Willoughby, wallaby, woo.
I don't know what to do.

Willoughby, wallaby, wee.
An elephant sat on me.

Willoughby, wallaby, wash.
I'm feeling kind of squash.

Willoughby, wallaby, woo.
And I don't know what to do

Lying on Things

After it snows
I go and lie on things.

I lie on my back
And make snow-angel wings.

I lie on my front
And powder-puff my nose.

I *always* lie on things
Right after it snows.

Rattlesnake Skipping Song

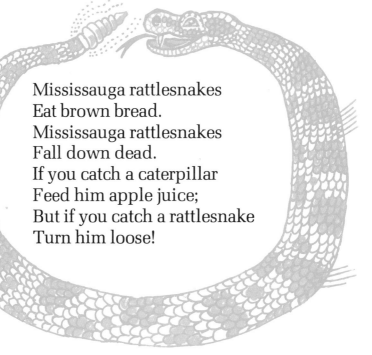

Mississauga rattlesnakes
Eat brown bread.
Mississauga rattlesnakes
Fall down dead.
If you catch a caterpillar
Feed him apple juice;
But if you catch a rattlesnake
Turn him loose!

Bed Song

Yonge Street, Bloor Street,
Queen Street, King:
Catch an itchy monkey
With a piece of string.

Eaton's, and Simpson's,
And Honest Ed's:
Give him his pyjama pants
And throw him into beds!

In Kamloops

In Kamloops
I'll eat your boots.

In the Gatineaus
I'll eat your toes.

In Napanee
I'll eat your knee.

In Winnipeg
I'll eat your leg.

In Charlottetown
I'll eat your gown.

In Crysler's Farm
I'll eat your arm.

In Aklavik
I'll eat your neck.

In Red Deer
I'll eat your ear.

In Trois Rivières
I'll eat your hair.

In Kitimat
I'll eat your hat.

And I'll eat your nose
And I'll eat your toes
In Medicine Hat and
        Moose Jaw.

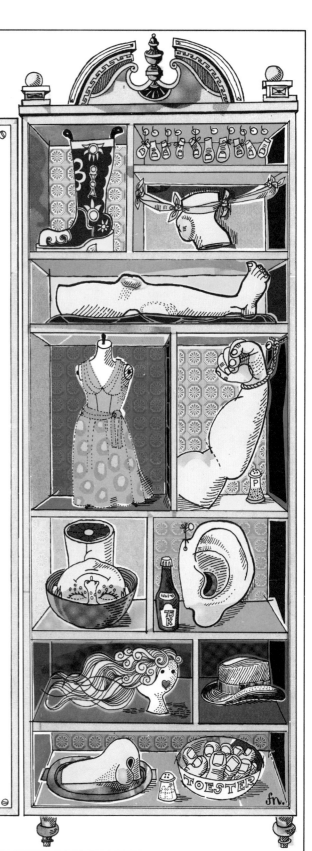

Billy Batter

Billy Batter,
What's the matter?
How come you're so sad?
I lost my cat
In the laundromat,
And a dragon ran off with my dad,
My dad—
A dragon ran off with my dad!

Billy Batter,
What's the matter?
How come you're so glum?
I ripped my jeans
On the coke machine,
And a monster ran off with my mum,
My mum—
A monster ran off with my mum!

Billy Batter,
Now you're better—
Happy as a tack!
The dragon's gone
To Saskatchewan;
The monster fell
In a wishing-well;
The cat showed up
With a new-born pup;
I fixed the rips
With potato chips,
And my dad and my mum came back,
Came back—
My dad and my mum came back!

Ookpik

An Ookpik is nothing but hair.
If you shave him, he isn't there.

He's never locked in the zoo.
He lives in a warm igloo.

He can whistle and dance on the walls.
He can dance on Niagara Falls.

He has nothing at all on his mind.
If you scratch him, he wags his behind.

He dances from morning to night.
Then he blinks. That turns out the light.

Bump on Your Thumb

Who shall be king of the little kids' swing?
Jimmy's the king of the little kids' swing
With a bump on your thumb
And a thump on your bum
And tickle my tum in Toronto.

Who shall see stars on the climbing bars?
Jimmy sees stars on the climbing bars
With a bump on your thumb
And a thump on your bum
And tickle my tum in Toronto.

And who shall come home with the night for his throne?
Jimmy's come home with the night for his throne
With a bump on your thumb
And a thump on your bum
And tickle my tum in Toronto.

The Special Person

I've got a Special Person
    At my day-care, where I'm in.
Her name is Mrs. Something
    But we mostly call her Lynn.

Cause Lynn's the one that shows you
    How to Squish a paper cup.
And Lynn's the one that smells good
    When you make her pick you up.
    She smells good when she picks you up.

She knows alot of stories
    And she reads them off by heart.
There's one about a Bear, but I
    Forget the other part.

She bit me on my knee once, cause I
    Said she couldn't scream,
And then I sent her in the hall,
    And then we had Ice Cream.

I guess I'm going to marry Lynn
    When I get three or four,
And Lynn can have my Crib, or else
    She'll maybe sleep next door,

Cause Jamie wants to marry Lynn
    And live here too, he said.
(I guess he'll have to come, but he's
    Too Little for a bed.)

Like a Giant in a Towel

When the wind is blowing hard
Like a giant in the yard,
    I'm glad my bed is warm;
    I'm glad my bed is warm.

When the rain begins to rain
Like a giant with a pain,
    I'm glad my bed is warm;
    I'm glad my bed is warm.

When the snowstorm starts to howl
Like a giant in a towel,
    I'm glad my bed is warm;
    I'm glad my bed is warm.

And when the giants realize
That no one's scared of their disguise,
They go to bed and close their eyes—
    They're glad their beds are warm;
    They're *glad* their beds are warm.

I'm stuck

Flying Out of Holes

Mr. Mole. Mr. Mole! MR. MOLE!!!
Come quick. I'm stuck in a hole.

Burrow along with your snout.
I'm stuck and I can't get out.

Push me and pull me. I'll pop
Straight up in the air, kerplop!

Aren't you going to come,
You no-good burrowing bum?

Never mind. I'm growing wings
To fly out of holes and things.

Now I'm flying straight up in the air.
When you get here, I'll land on your hair.

I flew right out of that hole.
Goodbye! Goodbye, Mr. Mole.

William Lyon Mackenzie King

William Lyon Mackenzie King
Sat in the middle & played with string
And he loved his mother like *anything*—
William Lyon Mackenzie King.

Tony Baloney

Tony Baloney is fibbing again—
Look at him wiggle and try to pretend.
Tony Baloney is telling a lie:
Phony old Tony Baloney, goodbye!

Skyscraper

Skyscraper, skyscraper,
Scrape me some sky:
Tickle the sun
While the stars go by.

Tickle the stars
While the sun's climbing high,
Then skyscraper, skyscraper
Scrape me some sky.

Tricking

When they bring me a plate
Full of stuff that I hate,
Like spinach and turnips and guck,
I sit very straight
And I look at the plate
And I quietly say to it: "YUCK!"

Little kids bawl
Cause I used to be small,
And I threw it all over the tray.
But now I am three
And I'm much more like me—
I yuck till they take it away.

But sometimes my dad
Gets terriffickly mad,
And he says, "Don't you drink from that cup!"
But he can't say it right
Cause he's not very bright—
So I trick him and drink it all up!

Then he gets up and roars;
He stomps on the floor
And he hollers, "I warn you, don't eat!!"
He counts up to ten
And I trick him again:
I practically finish the meat.

Then I start on the guck
And my daddy goes "Yuck!"
And he scrunches his eyes till they hurt.
So I shovel it in
And he grins a big grin.
And then we have dessert.

I Found a Silver Dollar

I found a silver dollar,
But I had to pay the rent.
I found an alligator
But his steering-wheel was bent.
I found a little monkey,
So I took him to the zoo.
Then I found a sticky kiss and so
I brought it home to you.

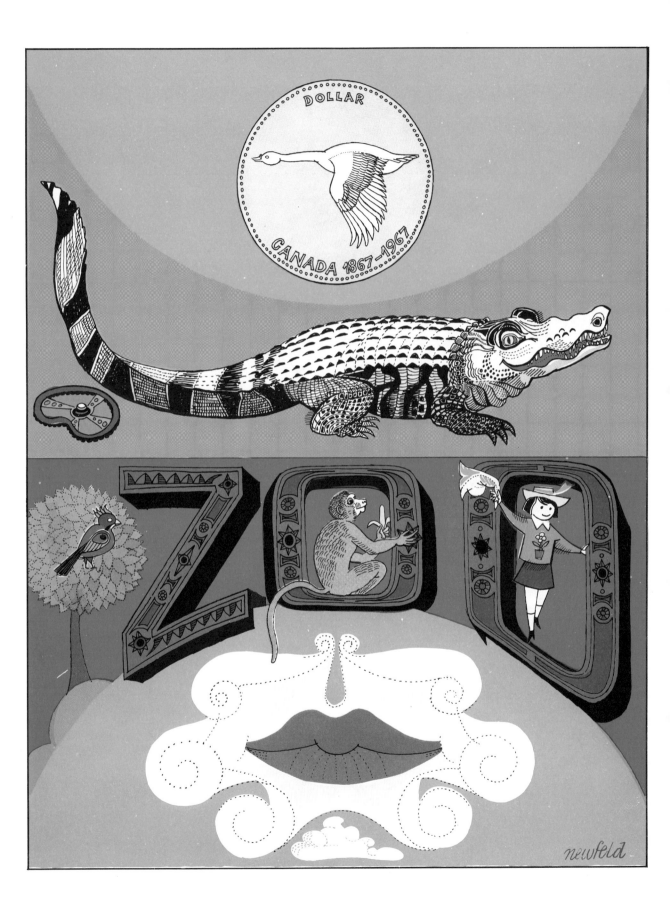

If You Should Meet

If you should meet a grundiboob,
Comfort him with sugar cubes.
Then send him on his way again
With feather beds, in case of rain.

If you meet him going out
Place a doughnut on his snout.
But if you meet him coming back,
Give his nose a mighty whack.

And if you meet a potamus,
Sleeping on a cotamus,
Do not sing or talkamus,
But take him for a walkamus.

If you should meet a crankabeast,
Be sure his forehead isn't creased;
Then pat him gently on his heads
And tuck him quickly into beds.

Higgledy Piggledy

Higgledy piggledy
Wiggledy wump,
I met a man
Who caught a mump:
With his left cheek lumpy
And his right cheek bumpy—
Higgledy piggledy
Wiggledy wump.

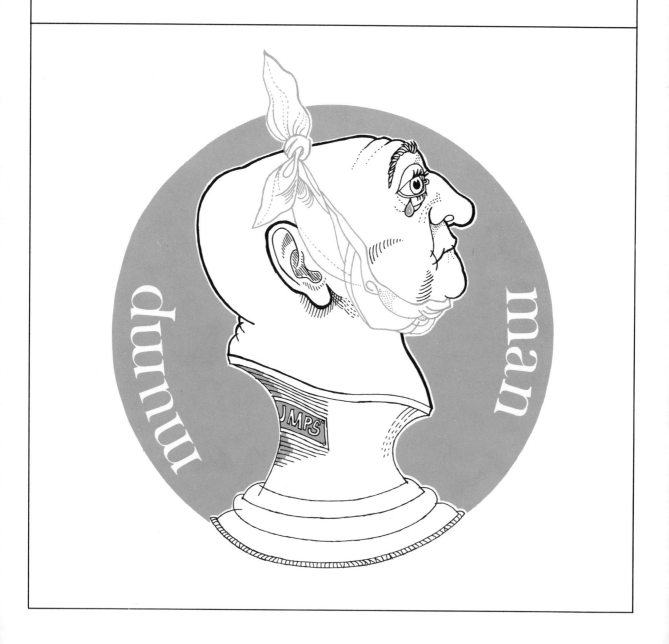

Higgledy piggledy
Sniggledy sneezle,
I met a man
Who caught a measle:
With his chest all dots
And his face all spots—
Higgledy piggledy
Sniggledy sneezle.

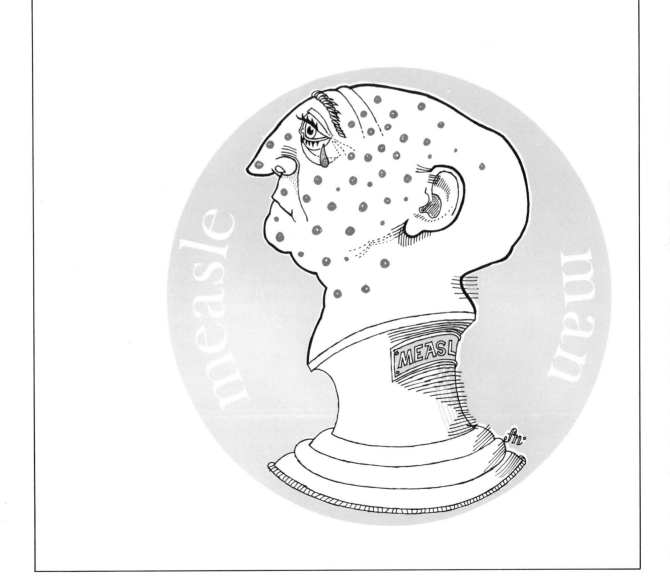

Thinking in Bed

I'm thinking in bed,
Cause I can't get out
Till I learn how to think
What I'm thinking about;
What I'm thinking about
Is a person to be—
A sort of a person
Who feels like me.

I might still be Alice,
Excepting I'm not.
And Snoopy is super,
But not when it's hot;
I couldn't be Piglet,
I don't think I'm Pooh,
I know I'm not Daddy
And I can't be you.

My breakfast is waiting.
My clothes are all out,
But *what* was that thing
I was thinking about?
I'll never get up
If I lie here all day;
But I still haven't thought,
So I'll just have to stay.

If I was a Grinch
I expect I would know.
I might have been Batman,
But I don't think so.
There's so many people
I don't seem to be—
I guess I'll just have to
Get up and be me.

Nicholas Grouch

Nicholas Grouch
Has filled his pouch
With garbage lids and bears.
When he gets home
His wife will groan
And throw him down the stairs.

more⟩

Nicholas Grouch
Has filled his pouch
With wet potato peelings.
When he gets back
His wife will yack
And hang him up on the ceiling.

Nicholas Grouch
Has filled his pouch
With licorice sticks and toffee.
When he gets in
His wife will grin
And give him a cup of coffee.

Psychapoo

Psychapoo,
The silly goose,
Brushed his teeth
With apple juice.

Psychapoo,
The melon-head,
Rode his bicycle
In bed.

His mother said,
"Sit down and eat!"
He swallowed the plate
And left the meat.

His father asked him,
"Can't you hear?"
He had a carrot
In his ear.

He met a dog
And shook its tail,
Took a bath
And caught a whale,

Put it in his
Piggy bank,
Said, "I think I'll
Call it Frank."

His brother asked him,
"Can't you see?"
He drank his hair
And combed his tea.

He took a trip
To Newfoundland,
Walking on water
And swimming on land

And every time
He heard a shout,
He took his pencil
And rubbed it out.

It isn't me,
It isn't you,
It's nutty, mutty
Psychapoo.

On Tuesdays
I Polish
My Uncle

I went to play in the park.
I didn't get home until dark.
But when I got back I had ants in my pants
And my father was feeding the shark.

I went to play in the park,
And I didn't come home until dark.
And when I got back I had ants in my pants
And dirt in my shirt, and glue in my shoe,
And my father was tickling the shark.

I went to sleep in the park.
The shark was starting to bark.
And when I woke up I had ants in my pants,
Dirt in my shirt, glue in my shoe,
And beans in my jeans and a bee on my knee,
And the shark was tickling my father.

My father went off to the park.
I stayed home and read to the shark.
And when he got back he had ants in his pants,
Dirt in his shirt, glue in his shoe,
Beans in his jeans, a bee on his knee,
Beer in his ear and a bear in his hair,
So we put him outside in the ark.

I started the ark in the dark.
My father was parking the shark.
And when we got home we had ants in our pants,
Dirt in our shirt, glue in our shoe,
Beans in our jeans, a bee on our knee,
Beer in our ear and a bear in our hair,
A stinger in our finger, a stain in our brain,
And our belly-buttons shone in the dark.

So my dad he got snarky and barked at the shark
Who was parking the ark on the mark in the dark.
And when they got back they had ants in their pants,
Dirt in their shirt, glue in their shoe,
Beans in their jeans, a bee on their knee,
Beer in their ear and a bear in their hair,
A stinger in each finger, a stain in the brain,
A small polka-dot burp, with headache tablets,
And a ship on the lip and a horse, of course,
So we all took a bath in the same tub and went to bed early.

The Fishes of Kempenfelt Bay

Under the bubbles
Of Kempenfelt Bay,
The slippery fishes
Dawdle all day.

They park in the shallows
And wiggle and stray,
The slippery fishes
Of Kempenfelt Bay.

I ride on a bike.
I swing in the gym.
But I'd leave them behind
If I knew how to swim

With the slippery fishes
That dawdle all day,
Under the bubbles
Of Kempenfelt Bay.

Kahshe or Chicoutimi

If I lived in Temagami,
Temiskaming, Kenagami,
Or Lynx, or Michipicoten Sound,
I wouldn't stir the whole year round

Unless I went to spend the day
At Bawk, or Nottawasaga Bay,
Or Missinabi, Moosonee,
Or Kahshe or Chicoutimi.

Tongue Twister

Someday I'll go to Winnipeg
To win a peg-leg pig.
But will a peg-leg winner win
The piglet's ill-got wig?

Someday I'll go to Ottawa
To eat a wall-eyed eel.
But ought a wall-eyed eater
Pot an eel that isn't peeled?

Someday I'll go to Nipigon
To nip a goony loon.
But will a goony nipper lose
His loony nipping spoon?

The Hockey Game

(With thanks to A. A. Milne)

Squirm
Was a
Worm
With a Terrible
Temper.
Wee
Was a flea
With a Big Bad Roar.
X
Was an elephant
Who couldn't keep his
Laces tied.
And **George** was a bit of a bore.

Squirm played
Hockey with a
Great big
Tooth-pick.
Wee played
Hockey with her
Friends and her foes.
X played
Hockey but he
Couldn't keep his
Laces tied.
And **George** just played with his toes.

Squirm threw a
Bodycheck and
Sent **X**
Flying.
Wee shot the
Puck and she
Knocked **X** flat.

X cried
Tears that were
Bigger than piano stools.
And **George** floated round in a hat.

Now
Squirm
Is a worm
With a Very
Soggy Temper.
And **Wee**
Is a flea
With a Waterlogged Roar.
X is an
Elephant who
Wonders where his
Skates went.
And **George** is rather wet
    George is *very* wet
    George is Awful wet
                  once
                    more.

Peter Rabbit

Peter Rabbit's
Mother sighed,
"Son, you'd better
Stay inside."

Peter Rabbit's
Father said,
"Don't you dare
Get out of bed!

"For if you do
You'll sneak away
And like a shot
You'll go and play

"In Farmer J.
MacGregor's garden—
Planning, without
A beg-your-pardon,

"To bolt his luscious
Turnips down
While we are shopping
In the town."

Peter yawned
At this to-do.
"So what?" he asked.
"You eat them too."

"It's not at all
The same," they said,
From either side
Of his messy bed,

"For since you will not
Use your spoon,
You'll turn into
A Spotted Goon!"

thank you, Miss Beatrix

2

"Shut up, dear parents."
Peter cried,
"You know I'd never
Sneak outside

"And wolf those luscious
Turnips down,
While you are shopping
In the town!"

Then Peter hummed
A loving hum,
And watched his tired old
Dad and mum

Teetering out
And tottering down
The steep steep hill
To the shops in town.

3

Then up he sprang
And off he sped
With visions of turnips
Alive in his head;

And up he rose
And off he ran
To where the turnip
Patch began.

He pulled up one.
He pulled up two.
He stuffed them in
And gave a chew.

And down they went
Kerplunk, because—
He crammed them in
With just his paws!

4

Then woe betide us!
Lack-a-day!
Good gosh, gadzooks and
Wellaway!

Quick, thick and fast
In inky blots
His fur broke out
With horrid spots.

He raced inside
To find a mirror;
The awful change
Grew clear and clearer:

Without a doubt
He was a Goon—
Because he *would* not
Use a spoon!

 5

Is this the end
Of Peter's tale?
A Goon-like life
In a spotted jail?

No, no! Again
I say it—No!
Great heavens! let it
Not be so!

For thinking of
His dreadful doom
He cried, "I Should Have
Used A Spoon!"

And pondering
His piteous plight
He roared, "My Dad
And Mum Were Right!"

At once his face
Began to shine.
He lit up like
A neon sign

Till someone put him
On T.V.
And parents forced
Their kids to see

The Shiny Spotted
Goody-Goon,
Who *Never* Ate
Without a Spoon.

Well, that's the story.
Here's the moral:
'Hare today
And Goon tomorrow.'

The Friends

When Egg and I sit down to tea
He never eats as much as me.
And so, to help him out I take
A double share of chocolate cake.
And when we get a special treat
He says he really couldn't eat—
Not even fudge, or licorice loops
Or butterscotch caramel ice-cream soup.
And likewise, if the juice is fine,
He always whispers, "Please drink mine."
And since Egg is my special friend
I gulp it down to the bitter end.
And Eggy says, when I hug him tight,
"I'm glad I had an appetite."

When Egg and I go out to play
His legs are always in the way,
And so he seems to fall alot
And always in a muddy spot.
And since Egg is my special friend
I fall down too; and I pretend
To cover myself with guck and dirt
So Eggy's feelings won't be hurt.
And when my mother starts to frown
I splain that Egg kept falling down,
And she throws us both in the washing machine,
And Eggy says, "I'm glad you're clean."

And when we go to bed at night
He sort of hates to shut the light.
He mentions, in a little voice,
"I hear a burglar kind of noise."
And also, "Giants scare me most."
And also, "That looks like a ghost!"
And since Egg is my special friend
I say that ghosts are half pretend.

I tell him everything's all right,
And I hide in the covers with all my might,
And then I get up and turn on the light.
And when the room is friends again
We snuggle down, like bears in a den,
Or hibernating in a cave.
And Eggy says, "I'm glad we're brave."

The Sitter
and the Butter
and the
Better Batter
Fritter

My little sister's sitter
Got a cutter from the baker,
And she baked a little fritter
From a pat of bitter butter.
First she bought a butter beater
Just to beat the butter better,
And she beat the bit of butter
    With the beater that she bought.

Then she cut the bit of butter
With the little butter cutter,
And she baked the beaten butter
In a beaten butter baker.
But the butter was too bitter
And she couldn't eat the fritter
So she set it by the cutter
    And the beater that she bought.

And I guess it must have taught her
Not to use such bitter butter,
For she bought a bit of batter
That was sweeter than the butter.
And she cut the sweeter batter
With the cutter, and she beat her
Sweeter batter with a sweeter batter
    Beater that she bought.

Then she baked a batter fritter
That was better than the butter
And she ate the better batter fritter
    Just like that.

But while the better batter
Fritter sat inside the sitter—
Why, the little bitter fritter
Made of bitter butter bit her,
Bit my little sister's sitter
     Till she simply disappeared.

Then my sister came to meet her
But she couldn't see the sitter—
She just saw the bitter butter
Fritter that had gone and et her;
So she ate the butter fritter
     With a teaspoonful of jam.

Now my sister has a bitter
Butter fritter sitting in her,
And a sitter in the bitter
Butter fritter, since it ate her,
And a better batter fritter
Sitting in the silly sitter
In the bitter butter fritter
     Sitting in my sister's tum.

Windshield Wipers

Windshield wipers
Wipe away the rain,
Please bring the sunshine
Back again.

Windshield wipers
Clean our car,
The fields are green
And we're travelling far.

My father's coat is warm.
My mother's lap is deep.
Windshield wipers,
Carry me to sleep.

And when I wake,
The sun will be
A golden home
Surrounding me;

But if that rain
Gets worse instead,
I want to sleep
Till I'm in my bed.

Windshield wipers
Wipe away the rain,
Please bring the sunshine
Back again.

Hockey Sticks and High-Rise: A Postlude

When I started reading nursery rhymes to my children, I quickly developed a twitch. All we seemed to read about were jolly millers, little pigs, and queens. The details of *Mother Goose* — the wassails and Dobbins and pipers and pence — had become exotic; children loved them, but they were no longer home ground.

Not that this was a bad thing. But I started to wonder: shouldn't a child also discover the imagination playing on things she lived with every day? not abolishing Mother Goose, but letting her take up residence among hockey sticks and high-rise too? I began experimenting.

I started with nursery rhymes. Later I made up poems for older children too; they're in the second half of this book, and in *Nicholas Knock and other people*. But I think I learned most from the nursery rhymes.

One thing I discovered is that the words should never be sacred. A rhyme is meant to be used, and that means changing it again and again. For children's verse passes around in weird and wonderful versions, and the changes always make sense — to the tongue and the ear, if not necessarily to the mind. If your child inadvertently rewrites some of these poems, please take his version more seriously than mine.

By the same token, you should feel free to relocate the place-poems as drastically as you want. Put in the streets and places you know best; the rhyme and the metre may get jostled a bit, but so what?

I also discovered that nursery rhymes can't be approached at an adult's reading rate. They unfold much more slowly. In fact, they need to be brought to life almost as tiny plays, preferably with much pulling of faces and bouncing of rear-ends on knees. One of these four-line poems may take a couple of minutes to complete, especially if you drop in new words and verses.

I had never realized how soon a child can take part in "doing poems". A two-year-old will join in, if you pause at the rhyme-word and let him complete it. Usually it will be the familiar rhyme, but if you're making up new verses you'll be surprised what he thinks of. Try starting a verse "Alligator juice", or "Willoughby wallaby wunk".

I hope the main thing I learned is invisible. There is a class of poem whose only virtue is that it Contains a Worthy Sentiment, or Deals With the Child's

Real World. Adults sometimes tolerate these wretched exercises, thinking they must be Literature. Young children, I can report, don't.

For I did commit a few of these pious versicles — highly Relevant poems about hockey players, developers, one about the CPR. They were awful, of course; wherever a poem comes from, it's not from good intentions. The undisguised boredom of my listeners persuaded me to pitch them out. And eventually I realized that the hockey sticks and high-rise would find their own way into the poem, without orders from me. My only job was to stop twisting their arms. Which is when it really got to be fun.

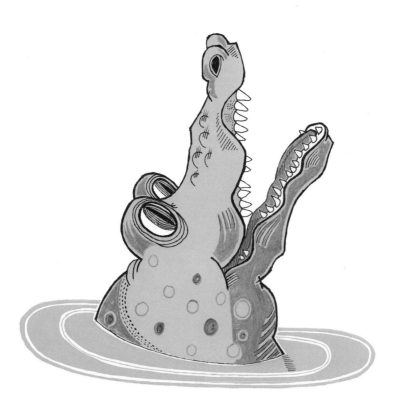